Puffin Book

Albert on the Farm

'What a glorious day!' remarked Albert Bear to the world in general, as he gazed out of the window of his basement home. 'That sky is just the colour of forget-me-nots and from the way my ears are tingling this morning, it's just the sort of day for something exciting to happen!'

And so it did! First of all, Digger, the koala bear from Australia, arrived for a holiday and then their old friend Mr Higgins asked them both to stay on the farm he was looking after for a week or two. What could be better? Albert and Digger were delighted. They had a wonderful time working on the farm, meeting all sorts of people and animals and doing lots of exciting things, like milking a cow and learning to make butter.

Another book by Alison Jezard

ALBERT
ALBERT'S CHRISTMAS

Alison Jezard

Albert on the Farm

Illustrated by Margaret Gordon

PUFFIN BOOKS

PUFFIN BOOKS

Published by the Penguin Group
27 Wrights Lane, London w8 5TZ, England
Viking Penguin Inc., 40 West 23rd Street, New York, New York 10010, USA
Penguin Books Australia Ltd, Ringwood, Victoria, Australia
Penguin Books Canada Ltd, 2801 John Street, Markham, Ontario, Canada L3R 1B4
Penguin Books (NZ) Ltd, 182–190 Wairau Road, Auckland 10, New Zealand

Penguin Books Ltd, Registered Offices: Harmondsworth, Middlesex, England

First published by Victor Gollancz Ltd 1979
Published in Puffin Books 1981
3 5 7 9 10 8 6 4

Made and printed in Great Britain by
Richard Clay Ltd, Bungay, Suffolk
Set in Linotype Pilgrim

FOR GRAEME
– second son of my daughter Hilary,
who first inspired Albert.

Contents

I

Albert's Visitor Arrives

'What a glorious day!' remarked Albert Bear to the world in general, as he gazed out of the window of his basement home. 'That sky is just the colour of forget-me-nots and from the way my ears are tingling this morning, it's just the sort of day for something exciting to happen!'

He set to work in a very happy mood. The lino on the floor was scrubbed and rubbed till it was shining clean. Mats were taken outside and shaken. The brass knobs on the old fender and the iron bedstead were polished and huffed on and polished again, and the summer sun peeped in the window to see what it was that was nearly as bright as *he* was.

Albert carefully dusted the marble clock, on the mantelpiece, that had belonged to his grandfather; then he climbed on a chair to wipe the picture of a sailing ship which hung over the fireplace.

'Whoops!' said Albert as the chair wobbled. He jumped down just in time.

He put clean sheets on the bed and smoothed down the bright patchwork quilt. Last of all, he set up his small folding bed in a corner.

Albert was expecting a visitor.

In the cupboard was a lovely chocolate cake with walnuts on it, a large jar of honey and some fat pink sausages, just waiting to pop in the pan and be fried golden brown.

The little bear was outside, sweeping the steps which led from Spoonbasher's Row down to his own front door at number fourteen, when he was startled to hear a wild yell.

'Cooooooeeeeeee! HI THERE, COBBER! COOOOOEEEEEE!'

Pounding down the street came a small furry bear, waving a bag in one paw and a bush hat in the other.

Digger, the koala bear from Australia, had arrived.

Albert was very pleased to see his friend and they tumbled excitedly down the steps into Albert's home, where Digger flopped breathlessly into one of the comfortable basket chairs.

'How long can you stay this time?' asked Albert, lighting the gas under the frying pan.

The koala bear worked on a ship which ran between England and Australia. He always visited Albert when he came into London docks, but it was usually only for a short time.

'I've got three weeks' leave,' Digger told him happily, 'but look, you don't want me here all that time. I can stay at the hostel.'

'You will not!' declared Albert, prodding the sausages indignantly with a fork. 'You're staying here with me.'

'Good on you,' said Digger, with a contented sigh.

Over the meal, which included half the cake

and several cups of tea, the bears chatted about all the things they had done since they had last been together.

When the table was cleared and the washing-up done, they decided to go and see Mr Higgins and Henry.

Down Spoonbasher's Row they strolled, in the afternoon sunshine, round the corner and into Candle Lane. Albert opened the door in the big gates, which had a sign over them saying HIGGINS JUNK YARD, and they went through into the clean-swept yard. There was no junk lying around these days because Mr Higgins had opened a small greengrocer's shop in the next street. As it was early-closing day, Henry the horse was out in the yard enjoying the sun and a bucket of oats and Mr Higgins could be seen through the open kitchen door, sitting at the table with a cup of tea. He was reading a letter and, when he saw the bears, he waved it at them and called, 'I'm glad you've come because I wanted a word with you.'

After stopping for a moment to speak to their great friend Henry, the bears went into the kitchen. They sat at the table and politely refused a cup of tea as they were much too full.

'This letter's from a friend of mine who has a small farm up in East Anglia,' Mr Higgins told them. 'You remember, Albert, you met them

once?' When Albert nodded he went on, 'Well, it seems Emma's been ill and Ted wants to take her to stay by the sea for a couple of weeks' rest and they want to know if I could go and look after the farm for them.'

'But do you know anything about farming?' asked Digger.

'I'll have you know, my lad, that I spent all my school holidays on a farm and then I worked on one for several years, till my father died and left me the junk business.'

'That sounds fine, Mr Higgins,' said Albert. 'Do you want me to look after the shop while you're away?'

'No, Albert, thank you for offering, but my young nephew has been working along with me, learning the trade, and he'll be all right by himself for a couple of weeks. No, I thought you two might like to come with me and have a spot of farm life. Milking the cows, feeding the chickens, haymaking, that sort of thing. What do you think?'

'I'd like that very much,' answered Digger, eagerly, 'but when are you going? I've only got three weeks.'

'The day after tomorrow; first thing Saturday morning, so that just fits in fine.'

Albert had not answered. He was sitting quite still with his mouth open and his eyes closed.

'How about you, Albert?' asked Mr Higgins again. 'Wake up! Do you want to come?'

Albert opened his eyes and a big grin spread over his face. He heaved a deep sigh of content-ment and finally said, 'Sorry, it's just that, when I got up this morning, I *knew* something good was going to happen today.'

'I take it you'd like to come then,' laughed Mr Higgins.

'*Yes, please!*'

'Well, that's settled.'

'Henry will be able to come too, won't he?' asked Albert. 'I know he'd love it.'

'Oh, yes, of course! He's as pleased as anyone. In fact, if we start off really early, we'll be able to go in the cart. It's much easier than the train anyway.'

'Never mind if I get worn out lugging you lot all
that way,' remarked the horse, from the doorway.

'Henry, you knew about this all the time and
you didn't say anything!' laughed Albert.

'I thought he was looking a tiny bit smug when
we came in,' said Digger.

'He always looks smug,' teased Mr Higgins,
'because he thinks he's so handsome.' Then, glancing at his watch, he went on, 'Now, we've got
things to do. There are some deliveries to make
and I must go round and speak to my nephew.'

'We can do the deliveries,' said Albert. 'Are
they all ready at the shop?'

'Could you? That would be a great help. Yes, they're ready and labelled. Here's the key. I'll see you back here later for some supper and to settle the details.'

Mr Higgins hurried off and the bears went out into the yard to harness the horse to the cart. Henry gave a deep sigh and pretended to feel very badly treated, but really he loved being fussed around by Albert. The little bear kept Henry's

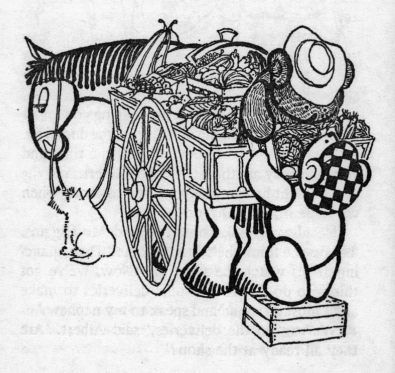

chestnut coat gleaming and the long hair of his mane and tail were always well combed. The horse would stand patiently while the bear cleaned dirt and stones out of the big hooves and, when new shoes were needed, the great shire horse would plod gently along behind Albert to visit their friend the farrier.

'Come on then, you great lazy thing,' cried Albert and Henry backed himself between the shafts of the cart. The bears fastened the harness and climbed on board.

Round at the shop they loaded up the boxes which had been left ready for delivery and for the next hour or so they drove round the narrow streets and lanes of East London, calling at houses to leave the orders of fruit and vegetables.

At last they were back at the yard and Mr Higgins could be seen setting the table for supper. Henry was unharnessed and, while Digger put the cart away, Albert settled Henry in his stable with oats and a bucket of fresh water.

'Good night, old lad,' said the little bear gently and Henry blew down Albert's neck, to show him how he felt about things, then tucked into his food.

In the kitchen, Mr Higgins told the bears that everything was arranged. His nephew would look after the shop and he had telephoned his friends to say that the three of them, with Henry, would arrive at the farm on Saturday afternoon.

They were just sitting down to their meal when they heard a very strange noise. They stopped to listen and realized that it was coming from the stable.

'It's Henry!' gasped Albert, jumping up. 'Is something wrong?'

'No, wait a minute,' said Mr Higgins. They listened and then he said, with a chuckle, 'He's all right!'

In fact, Henry was singing.

Into the summer evening the words came trilling:

> 'To plough and sow and reap and mow,
> And be a farmer's boy-oy-oy-oy-oy,
> And be a farmer's boy!'

2

Albert Starts Out

Mr Higgins and Henry were quite used to getting up very early to go to the fruit market and, when they called to collect Albert and Digger, the last tiny stars still shone faintly above the rooftops.

Two sleepy bears curled up, yawning, among the piles of luggage on the cart.

'I don't mind getting up at the crack of dawn,' muttered Digger. 'I just wish it wouldn't crack quite so early.'

Henry set off at a brisk trot and as they clattered and rattled through the empty streets the pearly-pink edges of day whispered into the sky.

By the time they were clear of the city the sun was high, promising another lovely summer's day. Mr Higgins turned the cart into a quiet side road and stopped in a shady spot where Henry could rest and crop the wayside grass. Digger spread a rug on the dew-wet ground and Albert unpacked the picnic basket he had brought.

'Do you know,' he remarked, setting out bacon

sandwiches and hard-boiled eggs, 'this is the first time I've ever been on a breakfast-time picnic. We should do this more often.'

They lingered over cups of tea from the thermos until Mr Higgins said, 'We'd better push on now, I can hear the traffic beginning to build up.'

Henry kept going steadily and he was very glad when they finally arrived and he turned the cart in through the open gate of a small farmyard.

Chickens fled from the wheels in a flurry of white feathers.

At one end of the yard was a pretty house with a thatched roof. Along one side stood the barn, a shed, the dairy and a garage. At the far end, a gate in the fence led to a large meadow where two red cows lay under the trees, chewing contentedly.

Ted and Emma came out of the house to greet them and Ted stroked Henry, saying, 'I've got a surprise for you. There's an old friend of yours here. You remember Brutus, don't you?' He opened the gate to the field and called to a horse in the far corner.

Henry suddenly let out a neigh of delight, reared up on his hind legs and dashed through the gateway, completely forgetting that he was still harnessed to a cart! A heavy wheel slammed into a stout gatepost and Henry came to a very abrupt halt. Albert, who had been standing on the cart unloading their luggage, landed on the back of his neck among the suitcases.

The big brown and white horse ambled over shaking his head. 'Same old Henry,' he said, 'still charging headlong through life!'

The two horses touched their soft noses to-

gether and then Brutus suggested, 'If you'd like to back up a bit, we'll get you sorted out.'

Henry backed out of the gateway and they found that the only damage was a few dents. 'Including one in my head,' complained Albert, rubbing it.

Henry was unharnessed and the two horses trotted into the meadow, where they were soon deep in conversation between mouthfuls of the sweet green grass that Henry missed so much in London.

The cart was unloaded and everyone went into the house, where a good meal was waiting for them.

'What made you buy a horse?' asked Mr Higgins, sitting down to the table.

'Well, like a lot of farmers these days, I decided that tractors are noisy things that use a lot of petrol and that I'd like to go back to the old-fashioned way of working.' He nodded towards a small, curly-haired dog that was asleep in a comfortable chair and went on, 'I only hope that Brutus turns out to be more use than Muffin. She's *supposed* to be a sheep dog.'

'Isn't she much use?'

'Well, put it this way, she's very enthusiastic! I wanted to call her Cornish Cream but Emma chose Muffin.'

'Why Cornish Cream?' laughed Albert.

'Because she's a bit of a clot!'

'I expect she'll be all right when she's older,' said Emma and, turning to Mr Higgins, she went on, 'It's very good of you to come and take over like this, at such short notice. I hope you won't have any trouble.'

'Now don't you worry about a thing,' Mr Higgins assured her. 'You just go off and have a good rest and get well again. We're looking forward to running the farm for you, aren't we, lads?'

Albert and Digger said they were very happy to be there and Digger promised to make sure the chickens were milked every morning!

'That's all right then,' chuckled Ted. 'Now why don't you two go and explore, if you've finished your meal, while we tell Mr Higgins a few things and get ready to go.'

'All right, come on then, Albert,' said Digger. At the open door he paused, looking out to where the farmland ran down to a narrow river that bubbled over stones and swept up again to a smooth round hill. 'Is it all yours? I mean the river and the hill?'

'Yes, the sheep graze on the hill and we get some good fishing in the river.'

'I was just thinking,' said the koala, 'what a

super hill that must be in the winter when it snows. It's perfect for tobogganing.'

'You're right,' agreed Emma. 'In fact, when the children were small, they used to come down that hill on a tin tray. I believe it's still in the shed, if you want to try.'

The bears prowled round the farmyard finding all sorts of exciting things. They peered into the gloomy barn, where sacks of grain were stored, and they heard the scampering of tiny feet.

'Mice?' suggested Albert.

'I expect so.'

The next building had four stalls for cows and behind lay a dairy, with cold stone slabs on which stood big, shallow dishes full of milk. Thick yellow cream had risen to the surface.

'Oh, gorgeous,' breathed Digger, dipping in a paw and licking off the lovely cream.

'You mustn't do that!' gasped Albert. But he could not resist the temptation to have one small lick. 'Mmm!'

In the shed they found the tractor and a lot of strange old farming tools they had never seen before.

'Here it is!' cried Digger, as he pounced on something in a dark corner. He showed Albert a stout, but rather rusty, tin tray. 'Come on, let's go and try it.'

A little puzzled about what it was that Digger wanted to do, Albert followed his friend out into the sunshine. They went through the yard gate,

across a small bridge over the river and then Digger began to climb the hill. By now Albert realized what Digger was up to, so he stayed at the foot of the hill where he could watch.

The koala climbed to the top of the hill, chose the right spot, sat down on the tray and pushed off. Slowly at first, and then with gathering speed, Digger came down the slope.

Everything went beautifully at first and then disaster struck! The tray hit a stone and parted company with the koala. The tray went off in one direction and Digger finished the trip on his tummy, arriving at Albert's feet breathless and laughing.

Collecting the tray and brushing the grass off his fur, Digger asked, 'Do you want to try?'

'No thanks,' laughed Albert, 'it's more fun watching you!'

Digger climbed back to the top and set off again, choosing a different way this time to avoid stones. The run went well until Albert suddenly realized what was going to happen.

'Oh, no!' he gasped, but there was nothing he could do.

Digger was heading straight for the river.

Sweeping gracefully down the hill, the koala sailed right over the grassy river bank and, still sitting on his tray, landed right in the middle of the cold bubbling water.

Albert could not help himself. He sat down on the ground and laughed till the tears rolled down his furry face.

With great dignity, Digger collected himself and the tray and waded out of the river.

Hiccoughing happily, Albert crossed the river by the more usual way of the bridge and joined his friend on the other side.

'Have you finished?' he chortled. 'Don't you want to go again?'

'No, thank you.'

Dripping, the koala made his way to the farm-house and a towel. 'Just you wait,' he muttered over his shoulder to the gurgling Albert, 'my turn will come.'

'Well, you've got off to a good start,' laughed Ted. 'We should have warned you about landing in the river!'

It was time for Ted and Emma to get going. They had arranged to drive down to the sea, stop-ping for the night on the way.

Mr Higgins and Ted loaded the luggage into the car, then the farmer and his wife were waved off on their holiday, with lots of good wishes.

'All right, now come on, you two, there's work to be done,' said Mr Higgins briskly, as the car disappeared round the corner.

The bears helped to feed the chickens and then shooed the clucking birds into their house, where they would be safe for the night.

As it was still summer and warm, the cows and horses could stay out in the meadow and Albert took some apples out for Henry and Brutus when he went to say good night.

The little white sheep grazed quietly on the hillside. They did not seem to have been at all disturbed by Digger's sledge run.

28

'Oooh!' yawned Albert, over a cup of bed-time cocoa. 'It's been a long day. I think I'll lie in for a bit tomorrow.'

'You'll be lucky!' laughed Mr Higgins.

'What do you mean?'

'Wait and see, lad. Just you wait and see!'

3
Albert Wakes Early

Next morning Albert saw exactly what Mr Higgins meant.

The two bears slept in a pleasant little room with roses peeping in the dormer window, right under the thatched roof of the farmhouse.

Albert was sound asleep in a snug nest of blankets and pillows when he slowly became aware that a new country day was beginning outside. He opened one eye sleepily and listened.

On the hillside the sheep were bleating to each other. The cows were calling to be milked and, of course, that was Henry joining in the chorus. Somewhere, a very noisy blackbird was arguing with his wife about the worm she had found. But what on earth was THAT!

Albert shot out of bed and ran to the window. Digger's head emerged with a bleary 'Huh?'

Mr Higgins threw open the door and called, 'Come on, you two, the farmyard alarm clock is telling you to get up!'

'It wasn't a clock I heard,' said Albert. 'What was it?'

'It was Percy. We call him the alarm clock. Look, there he is.'

Perched on the gatepost was a brightly-coloured bird. The jewel-green of his feathers glinted in the early sunlight. His proudly curling tail was black and the scarlet comb on his head quivered as he opened his beak and crowed to the morning once again.

'Well, do you know,' cried Albert, 'that's the first time I've ever heard a cock crowing.'

'I thought it might be. He doesn't think anyone else should sleep once he's awake! Come on, there's a cup of tea ready.'

From Digger's bed came muttering noises on the subject of noisy birds, but he climbed out of the blankets, grabbed his bush hat and followed the others downstairs.

'What's for breakfast?' he yawned.

'Nothing yet,' replied Mr Higgins. 'The animals come first on a farm. You'll be ready for breakfast after an hour or two's work.'

Digger said he was ready for it now but he went off quite willingly to let the chickens out, feed them and collect the eggs.

Albert went to help with the milking.

Mr Higgins brought in the two cows, whose

names were Sugar and Sweetheart, and tethered them in the stalls. They rolled their great brown eyes at Albert as he gave them a bundle of hay to chew while they were being milked.

Mr Higgins got the hosepipe, which led from a tap at the back of the shed, and gave the cows a good wash down. Then he fetched a clean bucket and the three-legged milking stool. Resting his shoulder and cheek against Sugar's warm, steaming flank, he began milking the cow, crooning gently to her as he did so.

Albert watched with great interest as the creamy-white milk flowed steadily into the pail. There seemed to be such a lot of it!

When Sugar was finished, Mr Higgins took the milk through to the cool dairy and came back with another bucket.

'Do you want to try?' he asked Albert.

'Yes, please.'

'Well, I'll just get her started and then we'll see what you can do.'

Mr Higgins milked Sweetheart for a few minutes and then stood up to show Albert how to hold the bucket and make the milk flow. He spoke soothingly to the cow and stroked her as she craned her head round to see what was going on.

The little bear did very well. Quite a lot of milk

was flowing into the bucket and he was feeling pleased with himself.

Mr Higgins looked pleased too and he started to say, 'But you must be careful that she doesn't move suddenly –' when Sweetheart stepped sideways and knocked Albert backwards off his stool. The pail tipped over him and he lay on the floor in a pool of fresh new milk.

Digger chose this moment to come in, carrying a basket of eggs. He looked down at his friend and then asked Mr Higgins, 'Wasn't it the Queen of

Sheba who used to bathe in milk every day to make herself beautiful?'

'Or was it Cleopatra?' replied Mr Higgins. 'Anyway, I know it was asses' milk not cows'.'

'Really! Still I expect it will do just as well.'

'I suggest,' chuckled Mr Higgins, 'that you get the hose and give him a wash.'

Digger was happy to oblige. He heaved Albert to his feet and turned the water on him. A few minutes later, Albert departed soggily towards the house.

By the time the cows were back in the meadow and the shed had been cleaned up, there was a delicious smell of frying bacon drifting out of the open door of the house.

They were just finishing what they all thought was a well-deserved meal, when a little blue van drove into the yard.

'Oh, that must be Sam come to collect the eggs,' said Mr Higgins. 'Look, we have to put this morning's eggs on to these trays.'

A big, cheery man came into the kitchen calling, 'Good morning. You must be our new farmers.'

After they had introduced themselves and Sam had drunk a cup of tea, the bears carried the trays of eggs out and put them in the back of the van.

'See you soon,' called Sam, as he drove off, and the bears turned back into the yard to see Mr

Higgins coming out of the shed carrying some tools.

'Come on,' he said, 'we're going hay-raking.'

The hay field lay beyond the meadow and they went out of the gate and down the lane to reach it. The bears carried big wide rakes with wooden teeth and Mr Higgins had a great curved knife on a long handle. He told them it was called a scythe.

They found that Ted had cut most of the hay and the pale golden grass lay drying in the sun.

'Now, while I get the last of it cut, you two turn the hay so that it dries underneath.'

With deep sweeping cuts of the scythe, Mr Higgins brought down the last of the standing hay, while the bears raked and tossed the sweet-smelling grass.

It was very pleasant working out in the fresh air, away from the noise and smell of London traffic.

Three pleasantly weary farm-workers plodded back down the lane at midday, waving to Brutus and Henry who were quite content to laze in their meadow and let others do the work.

After a good lunch, the bears were still full of energy.

'Well, if you're really *looking* for something to do,' said Mr Higgins, 'I see Ted has the white-wash ready to do the inside of the chicken house.'

'The *inside?*' answered Digger, in surprise.

'Yes, it's most important to keep everything which birds and animals use absolutely clean. Would you like to do it?'

Albert and Digger thought a job of whitewashing would be rather fun but Mr Higgins suggested that they had better leave their hats in the kitchen, in case they got them splashed.

First the bears cleared out all the old nesting material from the chicken house and gave the floor a good scrub. When this was finished, Mr Higgins arrived with the whitewash, ready mixed in a pail, and two broad brushes.

It certainly was fun sloshing away with the big brushes, slapping the wet wash on to the walls and ceiling, but they did it carefully and were pleased to see the wood dry quickly, looking clean and white.

The chickens clucked anxiously around, wondering what was going on and hoping they would be able to get back into their house in time to lay the evening eggs.

Even Percy strutted in and squawked around

complaining, but he was shooed out again by the busy bears.

'I only hope this stuff washes off,' commented Albert, as he reached up to a high place and the whitewash trickled down his arm.

'Don't worry if it doesn't,' replied the koala, 'it's a pretty pattern.' He himself had little white spots all over his face and ears.

'You look,' Albert told him, 'as if you have developed a new and interesting kind of measles.'

'Not measles,' laughed Digger, 'chicken-pox!'

Between the two of them, working hard with the big brushes, the job went quickly and, when Mr Higgins appeared at the door with a sack of clean straw for the nesting boxes, they had just about finished.

'You *have* done well,' he told them. 'It really does look clean and fresh. Ted will be very grateful to you.'

'We've enjoyed doing it,' said Albert, peering up into the corners. 'I wonder if we've missed anywhere.' He dabbed here and there with his brush, moving steadily backwards, hunting for bare patches, and looking in every direction except where he was going. So, of course, he bumped into the pail and knocked it over. The last of the whitewash shot out of the open door and slopped all over Mr Higgins' feet.

Albert gazed thoughtfully at the splattered boots.

'You could,' he suggested, 'start a new fashion. Whitewashed wellies!'

4
Albert Goes to Market

'You're a very nice little dog,' Albert told Muffin, 'but I don't think you'll ever be any good with sheep.'

Her feathery tail wagging with delight, Muffin jumped up and licked Albert's face.

'Down, Muffin. Sit.'

The little dog grinned happily.

'Sit!' repeated Albert firmly.

Muffin sat. For about ten seconds. Then she was off again, excitedly running amongst the sheep, barking at them in sheer high spirits.

'You're supposed to be rounding them up,' shouted Mr Higgins, 'not scattering them. Come here, Muffin.'

Whatever else Muffin did or did not do, she always came when she was called. She hurled herself at Mr Higgins joyously and nearly knocked him flying.

Mr Higgins put the dog's leash on her and handed it to Albert. 'Lead her round,' he said, 'and show her how it's done.'

It was early evening and next morning a neighbouring farmer would be calling with his lorry to collect six of the sheep and take them to market. Ted had arranged to sell them to pay for the winter feed for the cows and chickens.

Mr Higgins had set up a pen made of hurdles and, now that the sheep had come down off the hillside to drink at the river, he and the bears were trying to round them up and pick out the six marked ones. Muffin was supposed to be helping, but her idea of rounding up sheep was to dive right into the middle of the flock and scatter them in all directions. She thought it was all great fun and barked happily.

With Muffin now firmly on her lead and told to keep quiet, they managed to gather the sheep together and find the six for market. Mr Higgins heaved them into the pen and let the others go. They scrambled rapidly up the hill to safety.

'Thank goodness that's done,' gasped Albert, slipping Muffin's lead. She disappeared into the barn, having decided that rounding up mice was more fun.

The three of them strolled gently over the bridge and stopped to gaze into the waters of the river which sparkled in the evening sunlight.

'Let's get a rod and do some fishing,' suggested Albert.

'No need for a rod,' replied Digger, peering intently into the shadow of a big stone. 'Just watch me.'

The koala crept silently down the grassy bank and lay flat at the edge of the river. Very slowly and carefully he slid his paw into the water and waited, hardly breathing. Albert followed quietly and stood watching.

Suddenly Digger jerked his paw out of the water. A silvery fish shot through the air and hit Albert smack on the ear.

'Grab it!' yelled Digger, as the fish flopped on to the grass and lay there jerking and gasping.

Albert pounced and missed. The fish gave a

violent twist, fell back into the river and quickly disappeared.

'Oh, bother!' grunted Digger, disappointed. 'I was going to have that for my supper.'

'If you'll settle for Irish stew, it should be ready by now,' said Mr Higgins.

Early next morning the lorry came up the lane and parked by the bridge. Leaving Muffin in the house, the three brought the penned sheep across the bridge and loaded them into the back of the lorry where there were eight other sheep, also bound for market. One did his best to escape back up the hill but was chased by the bears and pushed in beside his companions. Then the two breathless bears loaded themselves into the front seat. They were off to market, leaving Mr Higgins to do some more hayraking.

When they arrived at the nearby town and turned into the big gates of the market area, the farmer parked by the sheep pens and was told where to unload. He dropped the tailgate of the lorry and shooed the sheep out. As they came piling out into their selling pen, in amongst them, with a silly grin on her face, was Muffin!

'Oh no,' groaned Digger. 'Here, hold my hat, Albert, while I get her out.'

He handed his bush hat to Albert and climbed into the pen. He was burrowing among the sheep, trying to get hold of the dog, when a farmer came up.

'That's a funny coloured sheep,' he remarked and prodded with his stick.

'OUCH!' yelped Digger, straightening up suddenly.

'I'm very sorry,' muttered the astonished farmer.

'I'm not for sale,' said Digger, indignantly, climbing out of the pen with Muffin.

'Oh, I don't know,' murmured Albert. 'Make

me an offer. As a matter of fact, you can have the pair of them for a couple of pounds. They'd be quite – er – perhaps not,' he finished, catching sight of his friend's face. 'Do you happen to have a piece of string in your pocket?' he asked, changing the subject.

The farmer produced a stout piece of cord and Albert tied it to Muffin's collar saying severely, 'Now just try and behave yourself.'

It was time for the sheep sales to begin. The auctioneer, the man responsible for the selling, had arrived. The bears were most interested in the way the group of sheep farmers worked their way very quickly round the pens. Each man knew just which animals he wanted to buy and the auctioneer sold to the man who bid the highest amount. Albert and Digger were delighted when Ted's sheep were sold for a very good price.

It was at the last pen that Albert made his mistake. The auctioneer was rapidly building up the price, glancing all the time round his audience. Finally, he called, 'Sold to the bear in the checked cap. Right, that's all thank you, gentlemen.'

Albert looked all round for the bear in the checked cap and then he suddenly realized. 'Hey!' he shouted. 'I don't want to buy any sheep. I'm selling, not buying.'

The auctioneer turned back, 'But you scratched

your nose,' he said. 'I thought you were making a bid.'

'I scratched my nose because it was itchy, not because I wanted to buy anything,' protested Albert.

There was a good deal of laughter at this and the sheep were sold to a farmer who really wanted them.

The bears decided not to go to the cattle sale, in case they found themselves taking home a large bull. Instead they wandered round the whole market area, looking at the cages of small birds, pigeons, rabbits, puppies and kittens. Albert very badly wanted to buy a fluffy white rabbit but Digger persuaded him not to.

'He'd have to live in a hutch,' said the koala, 'and you know you wouldn't like that. You couldn't let him loose in London,' and Albert had to agree.

They looked at the stalls where dress materials and ornaments and all sorts of things were set out for sale and Albert cried, 'Oh look, Digger, doughnuts!'

They stood watching at a stall while a man dropped rings of creamy dough into deep fat, where they bobbed about sizzling and bubbling. When they were golden-brown they were scooped out and rolled in sugar.

Albert bought a bagful and they strolled on, enjoying the hot, fresh doughnuts and sharing them with Muffin.

'We'd better get back to the lorry now,' said Digger, licking sugar off his paws.

The farmer was waiting for them and they were soon back home again where they found Mr Higgins chatting with Henry and Brutus, at the meadow gate. When Albert told them the story of how a farmer nearly bought Digger, Henry looked the little koala up and down. 'Personally, I think you missed a good opportunity there,' he remarked, gloomily. Albert glanced at his big friend in surprise. The horse was standing with his head hanging down, not looking at all happy.

Albert produced his bag of doughnuts and said, 'Look, I've saved you one each. Here you are, Henry, you'll like this.'

'No, thank you,' murmured the horse.

'Henry,' said Albert anxiously, 'aren't you well?'

The horse raised his head, looked sorrowfully at the little bear and said, 'It hurts.' Then, to everyone's horror, he suddenly lay down on the grass and closed his eyes.

Mr Higgins took one startled look at the still horse and raced to telephone for the vet.

It seemed a terribly long wait.

Albert sat on the grass and stroked Henry's soft nose. Digger found a small leafy branch and fanned away the irritating flies. Mr Higgins stood around unhappily, making soothing noises, and Brutus nuzzled his friend, whinnying anxiously.

A car came up the lane and the vet strode quickly over. He asked Mr Higgins a few questions and then he examined Henry.

After a few minutes he stood up and said, 'So he's really a London horse. He doesn't get out into the country much?'

'That's right.'

'And he doesn't often get the chance to eat grass?'

'No, but he eats it whenever he can. He likes it very much.'

'Yes, well I'm afraid,' said the vet, 'that's just the trouble. He's liked it a bit *too* much this time. He's been over-eating and got a touch of colic. But don't worry, it's a very mild attack, though it's making him feel pretty bad.'

Henry raised his head and agreed pathetically that he did feel bad and if this was a 'mild attack' he hoped he would never have a bad one.

'Be more careful with the grass and you probably won't,' the vet told him, stroking the horse's neck. 'Now,' he said, 'if we could get the lad under

cover for the night, I'll give him an injection and I'm pretty sure he'll be fine in the morning.'

With a bit of help, Henry staggered to his feet and limped painfully into the barn. The bears quickly made him a comfortable straw bed and he collapsed gratefully on to it. The vet opened his bag and took out a hypodermic needle. He gave Henry the injection and then, gathering his things together, he said, 'Now, you call me at once if you think he's any worse, but I'm sure he won't be. Good-bye, old chap, and just you remember about the grass.'

'I never want to see grass again as long as I live,' muttered Henry feebly.

'Do you want to bet?' smiled Mr Higgins.

5
Albert and the Bees

Next morning Henry had completely recovered.

Albert slept in the barn, to take care of him, sharing the straw bed and a couple of blankets.

Percy made his usual alarm call from the gate-post and then strutted into the barn to make sure the sleepers in there did not go on sleeping. He fluttered on to a bale of straw near Albert's head and let loose a specially good crow. The little bear shot out of bed yelping, 'Don't do that in my EAR!'

Percy went off in a huff. It was his job to make sure nobody overslept and he did not expect to be shouted at for doing it.

Albert brushed bits of straw off himself and found his cap.

'How are you feeling today?' he asked, gently.

Henry climbed carefully to his feet, took a few steps, shook himself and announced in a surprised voice, 'I feel fine! But I'm thirsty.'

Happily, Albert dashed off and came back with a bucket of fresh water.

Would you like some breakfast?'

'I think I might just nibble a carrot.'

In fact, he nibbled two carrots and Albert said he had better not have any more until the vet had seen him.

'Now you just stay quietly in here while I go and do the milking.'

Breakfast, in the kitchen, was nearly over when the telephone rang. Mr Higgins went to answer it.

'Yes, that's fine. Whenever you like. I expect Emma forgot to tell me but it's quite all right. Yes,

they'll probably want to help you, as long as they won't be in your way. See you later, then.'

Mr Higgins put down the phone, went back to his cup of tea and then, very casually, he told the bears, 'That was Sam. He just called to say he'll be round this morning to get the honey from the bees.'

There was a moment's astonished silence.

'Bees?' murmured Albert.

'Honey?' breathed Digger.

'Yes, haven't you noticed the hives in the garden?'

Since Albert and Digger had been at the farm, they had been so busy with one thing and another that they had hardly been in the enclosed garden that lay behind the house. Now they dashed off down the side path to the garden and the vegetable patch behind.

They went through a gap in the tall hedge and along a crazy-paving path that led between beds full of brightly coloured flowers. There were lupins, delphiniums, snapdragons, hollyhocks and sunflowers and everywhere there were bees. The scented garden *hummed* with bees.

Against the far hedge stood four square white hives. It was fascinating to watch the fat little golden-striped insects come creeping out of the narrow slits at the bottom of the hives and go swirling off, to fuss busily round the flowers, in and out, and then come bumbling back, laden with yellow pollen to make into gorgeous honey for lucky bears.

The bears could have stood watching for hours but they heard Mr Higgins calling them and ran back to the farmyard to find that the vet had arrived.

Henry was examined and declared quite fit again but he was to eat very little for a day or two.

'Now you take care of yourself, do you understand,' said the vet severely to the horse, stroking

his neck. 'We can't have a splendid-looking lad like you making yourself ill again.'

Henry trotted smugly off to the field where Brutus was waiting for him. The first thing he did was to roll on the grass, his legs kicking in the air. Then he set off on a mad canter round the meadow, with Brutus chasing after him and the cows dashing out of the way.

'Not much wrong with him now,' laughed the vet. 'I love these beautiful great shire horses, don't you?'

Albert agreed that Henry was a lot more fun than a fluffy white rabbit.

When the vet had gone, Albert and Digger helped Mr Higgins with odd jobs around the farm, but there always seemed to be at least one of them hovering anxiously round the gate, peering up the lane, watching for the little blue van.

At last Sam arrived and, as he unloaded his gear, he did not seem to be in the least surprised to find that every move he made was closely watched by two small bears.

The honey-extracting machine was unloaded and set up in the scullery behind the kitchen. Then, from a box, Sam took out a wide-brimmed hat, with a veil that covered his face and tucked into his collar, and a pair of heavy gloves.

'You'd better keep well back, in case you get stung,' he told them.

'They won't sting us,' Albert assured him.

'Are you sure?'

'Quite sure.'

'Well, come on then.'

The three honey-hunters went round into the garden. Sam lifted the top off the first hive and was immediately surrounded by furious bees, attacking the thief who was stealing their precious honey.

'But if you take all their honey, what will they live on?' asked Digger.

'Don't worry, we'll leave them a little for now and in the winter Emma will feed them with sugar syrup.'

Sam took a large wooden frame from the hive and, after gently sweeping the clinging bees from it, he showed it to the bears.

Albert and Digger had, of course, always known that bees get pollen from flowers and make it into honey, but this was the first time they had ever seen the wonderful way the little insects made six-sided wax cells that all fitted together, were filled with honey, and then sealed with more wax.

'Where do they get the wax?' asked Albert, and was astonished to learn that the bees actually made it inside their own bodies and squeezed it out in tiny sheets!

Brushing a peevish bee off his nose, Digger peered into the hive.

'Where's the queen bee?'

'She's on a lower layer and we mustn't disturb her or she might get upset and fly off, taking the whole swarm with her and Emma wouldn't like that!'

The frames were carried into the scullery where, with a hot knife, Sam scraped the wax off one side of the cells. Then they were put into the extractor and spun round very fast. The spinning pulled the honey out in just the same way that a spin-dryer pulls the water out of clothes.

It was quite a long job and, half-way through, Mr Higgins called them in to dinner. On the table stood a steaming roast chicken.

Digger was about to tuck hungrily into his share when he stopped suddenly.

'This isn't one of ours, is it?' he asked anxiously.

'No, lad,' laughed Mr Higgins, 'but if you want to be a farmer, you'll have to learn to eat the food you produce, whatever shape it's in. But you needn't worry, this one came from a farm up the road.'

'That's all right then,' replied the koala, 'just as long as it's a stranger.'

The bears agreed later that it was one of the best days they had ever spent. Backwards and forwards they went, fetching the frames, scraping off the wax, spinning out the honey and getting steadily stickier and stickier.

At last, all the honey had been gathered and Sam put it into a big pan on the stove to get hot. 'That makes it more runny,' he explained, 'so that we can strain it through muslin to get all the bits out.'

'Shall we scrub the frames clean?' asked Albert.

'Oh, no, the bees will do that. The last thing we do is to put the frames back in the hives, just

as they are, and the bees will eat all the wax and honey off them and make them quite clean. That way they get food to start the job all over again.'

By tea-time the honey had been strained and left to settle in a deep bowl.

'Tomorrow you can pour it into those screw-top jars and put them into Emma's store-cupboard,' Sam told the bears.

When everything had been cleaned up and put away, they went into the kitchen, Albert proudly carrying a piece of honeycomb on a plate. Sam had saved it for them because they had never eaten it straight from the comb before.

They found that Mr Higgins had not been idle. The most delicious smell of hot fresh scones greeted them.

It was a little strange to cut a chunk of comb and eat the tiny wax cells along with the honey but, spread on hot scones dripping with butter, it was marvellous.

'Bliss!' murmured Albert, a trifle indistinctly.

6

Albert Goes Haymaking

Days on the farm passed all too quickly and very pleasantly. Although there was quite a lot of work to be done, with the three of them they managed

easily and had plenty of spare time to enjoy themselves.

Percy made quite sure they were all up and about very early every day.

Digger had taken over the job of looking after the chickens. He had given them names and now they came when he called instead of having to be chased and shooed around. Even Percy condescended to take corn from the koala's paw.

Albert was now an expert dairyman, or dairybear. He milked the cows morning and evening and, after putting milk aside for the house, he set the rest of it in the wide, shallow pans. After these had been standing for some hours, all the thick yellow cream lay on the surface. Albert carefully scooped off the cream and the skimmed milk went into churns to be collected by a local pig-farmer.

It was an exciting day when Albert made his first butter. He saved the cream for two days and put it into the butter-churn, which was like a small barrel resting sideways on a stand. He fastened the lid and began to turn the handle. The churn spun steadily round, with the little bear constantly lifting the lid to peer inside and see if anything was happening yet. It seemed to take forever but, suddenly, there it was. The cream had turned into rich golden butter! Albert washed it in cold water to take off the excess milk and carried it proudly into the kitchen. It *did* taste good.

Later Mr Higgins showed him how to use the

pats and moulds that hung on the dairy walls.
After that, every time Albert made butter, he carefully shaped it with the ribbed wooden pats and
pressed on to it a hollow mould, which left the
shape of a thistle or a crown. Sometimes Albert's
butter looked almost too good to eat!

It was their second to last day when Mr Higgins
looked out at a strangely brassy-looking sky and
said, 'I think we're in for some thunder. We'd
better get the hay in today, or it might be
spoilt.'

So Brutus was hitched to the high-sided farm
cart and, armed with rakes and pitchforks, they
went off to the hayfield.

It was hot, dusty work but they kept at it
steadily, raking the hay into heaps and forking it
up on to the cart which Brutus pulled round to
the barn. He backed through the big doorway and
the hay was stacked in a dry corner.

On one trip back to the farm, Albert went into
the kitchen and made a pile of cheese sandwiches,
which he took back to the field along with a jug of
milk.

They sat in the shade of a tree with their picnic
and Henry hung over the hedge sharing Albert's
sandwiches.

'It's all very well,' complained the bear, 'but I
don't eat your grass.'

'You're very welcome, there's plenty of it around, especially since I've had to cut down on it.'

'Thanks very much!'

'Shush, keep still,' said Mr Higgins, suddenly.

Everyone stopped breathing for a moment and watched as he peered at a pile of hay. Then he pounced and came up with cupped hands. Slowly, he opened them and there, sitting in his palm, was a tiny creamy-brown mouse.

'It's a field mouse,' he told them.

'It's so small, it just doesn't seem possible,' breathed Albert.

Digger broke off a crumb of cheese and held it out to the little creature. A tiny black nose twitched, then the mouse took the cheese daintily in its paws and began to nibble.

Very carefully, Mr Higgins put the mouse into the safety of the hedgerow where it made a dive and disappeared.

Lying back on the hay, peacefully smoking his pipe, Mr Higgins said to Brutus, 'I see the plough's over there. I've always wanted to try my hand at ploughing and I know Ted wants his field turned over.'

'Well, I've done plenty of it,' replied the horse. 'We can give it a try.'

So, when the last of the hay had been stored in

the barn, Brutus was taken out of the cart and hitched to the plough. Mr Higgins took a firm grip of the two handles and they started along the edge of the field.

At first Mr Higgins found it very difficult to keep the heavy plough in place. The big curved blade was not cutting into the ground properly but, with some patient advice from Brutus, he began to get the hang of it and the second furrow was much better, though not very straight.

Turning the plough behind the horse at each end was tricky, but the bears helped, and soon it was turning easily and the furrows were getting deeper and straighter.

'Hey, I'd like to have a go at that,' called Henry, from the meadow. 'I'm coming over.' He trotted back to give himself room.

'Henry!' yelled Mr Higgins. 'Come round. DON'T JUMP!'

But it was too late. Henry was already cantering up to the hedge.

What happened next no one was ever quite sure, least of all Henry.

One moment he seemed all set for a splendid leap and the next he had landed smack on top of the hedge, with his hind legs in the meadow and his front legs in the hayfield.

'Henry,' said Brutus sadly, 'we shire horses are

just not built for steeple-chasing. I hope you haven't damaged yourself.'

'I don't *think* so.'

'Well you've certainly damaged the hedge,' Mr Higgins told him severely.

A wriggle, a squirm, an almighty heave, and Henry managed to get all four feet back in the same field.

'I'll come round,' he said and trotted away, leaving the others to repair the damaged hedge.

When he arrived in the hayfield, Henry was hitched to the plough in place of Brutus.

'Now, take it steady,' commanded Mr Higgins, 'and don't do any of your wild charging around.'

Henry did his best to plod along carefully and gently, as he had seen his friend do, and, to everyone's surprise, he did very well, keeping to a straight line with a steady pull on the plough.

Then, of course, everyone had to have a go and it developed into a competition to see which team did the best. They had just decided that Brutus and Digger had ploughed the three straightest, deepest furrows when the sky was ripped apart by the most tremendous flash of forked lightning.

'It's going to pour,' cried Mr Higgins. 'You two go and see to the cows and chickens. I'll look after Brutus and Henry.'

Great dark swirling clouds were racing over the

hill and the sun disappeared as if it had been switched off.

The bears raced away, Albert to the meadow to bring in Sweetheart and Sugar who were looking a bit scared, while Digger ran around gathering up his panicky chickens.

Percy flew on to the barn roof and crowed defiantly at the lowering sky, but a flash of lightning, followed by a deep roll of thunder, sent him fluttering for cover.

The horses clattered quickly home and sheltered in a warm corner of the barn. Mr Higgins gave them both a good rubdown and an armful of the sweet new hay.

By the time he had finished, the rain was lashing down and the thunder crashed right overhead. It was quite frightening but the bears were too busy to worry about it. Digger got his white chickens, now a bit muddy and wet, settled into their house with plenty of chicken feed and then galloped across the yard, carrying the evening's collection of eggs, just as Albert came charging out of the dairy to fetch an extra ration of hay for his precious cows.

They met head-on and Digger's basket went flying.

'Scrambled eggs, anyone?' murmured Mr Higgins. He picked the bears up and suggested that they really would not get any wetter if they just took things a little more slowly.

The broken shells were swept up and the rain quickly washed away the rest of the mess. The bears finished their work more carefully.

They were all very wet by the time they gathered in the kitchen and Mr Higgins was just building up a nice, cheerful wood fire when there was

the most terrible flash of lightning, followed by a very loud bang, a dreadful tearing, splintering noise and the most awful crash.

They stood quite still, staring at each other, with their mouths open.

Then Mr Higgins said, in a scared whisper,

'Something's down. I hope it isn't the barn.'

'Or the dairy,' gasped Albert.

'Or the CHICKEN HOUSE!' yelped Digger and they raced into the teeming rain to find out what had happened.

With the water lashing into their faces, it was hard to see anything, but all the buildings seemed to be undamaged. The cows were safe though frightened and the horses were stamping their feet a bit, but making 'don't worry about us' noises.

Searching further for the cause of the crash,

they struggled against the storm up to the meadow gate.

'There it is,' shouted Mr Higgins into the wind and pointed. In the far corner of the field a great elm tree, the one the cows and horses liked to stand under, was lying on its side, its roots waving wildly at the sky.

It looked awful but there was nothing they could do, so they fought their way back to the kitchen.

The storm raged. The wind howled. The rain teemed and streamed.

But now everyone was sheltered and fed, warm and dry.

'I just hope Ted isn't going to be too upset about that tree,' said Mr Higgins.

7
Albert the Shepherd

The storm raged round the farm till the early hours and the morning dawned dismal and drizzly. Even Percy was late getting up. However, by the time breakfast was sizzling in the pan, the sun had relented. It pushed the clouds out of the way and burst out in its full glory.

'Ted and Emma will be home in time for supper,' said Mr Higgins. 'I'm going to spend the day tidying up the garden and the vegetable patch.'

'Keep an eye on the bees,' Digger told him. 'We don't want them slacking off.'

'What would you like us to do?' asked Albert.

'Well, I know it would be a great help to Ted if you could pick the plums on that big tree by the meadow gate. I know Digger's very good up trees. There's a ladder in the shed.'

'I shan't need a ladder,' replied Digger, airily. 'Koalas can climb *any* tree.'

'Well, *I'll* use the ladder,' said Albert.

In the shed they also found two canvas bags to

carry over their shoulders and a big wooden fruit box.

After helping to prop the ladder against the tree, Digger said, 'You pick the lower branches and I'll go up to the top.'

'Be careful,' said Albert but the koala waved the warning aside and, digging his claws into the bark of the old tree, he shinned straight up and disappeared among the leaves.

The deep-red plums were just ripe and ready to pick and not all of them went into the bags. Every now and then one of the busy fruit-pickers paused to dig his teeth into the soft golden flesh and wipe the juice off his chin with his paw.

Up and down the tree they went for most of the morning and Albert had to go and get another box.

At last he climbed down the ladder and called up the tree, 'I'll just go and ask Mr Higgins to give us a hand with these heavy boxes. I expect you're pretty well finished up there.'

The answer was a grunt and the rustle of leaves.

Albert laid the ladder on the grass and went round to the garden. He found Mr Higgins cutting off dead flower heads and stayed to help.

After a while Mr Higgins straightened up and said, 'There, that'll do for this morning. I'll just help you with those boxes before we eat.'

Back at the meadow the boxes of plums lay on

the grass by the tree but there was no sign of the koala.

'Digger!' called Albert but there was no answer.

Henry plodded over and put his head down by Albert's ear.

'Don't look now, but I think he's stuck up that tree.'

'He can't be, he's supposed to be so good at climbing.'

'Well, he *is* good but I still think he's stuck.'

Albert went over to the tree and called up, 'Are you all right, Digger?'

'I'm bonzer, cobber. I'll be down in a minute.'

Albert and Mr Higgins looked at each other and at the ladder on the ground.

'He'll never admit he's stuck,' whispered Albert. 'What can we do?'

Mr Higgins gazed up the tree, then he suddenly said, 'Look, Albert, see that hole in the trunk about halfway up?'

Albert peered. There did not seem to be any hole.

'Yes, look, I'm sure it's a woodpecker's nest. I'm going up to see.'

Mr Higgins rested the ladder against the tree, as near as he could to where he thought Digger was. He climbed up a short way, chatting all the time

about birds' nests. Then he came down again and said, 'Right, let's get this fruit indoors. I'll come back for the ladder later.'

The two of them went off, carrying a box between them, and Henry retired, tactfully, to the other side of the field.

There was a mighty rustling in the top of the tree. Leaves and twigs fell to the grass. Down the ladder crept Digger, looking all round him to see if anyone was watching.

From behind the kitchen curtain, Mr Higgins and Albert had a good chortle. Then they straightened their faces and went back for the second box.

'Oh, hello there, Digger,' said Albert casually. 'Is that the last of the plums?'

'That's it,' replied the koala, emptying his bag into the box. 'Dinner ready?'

When early evening came, it brought Ted and Emma. They climbed out of the car and gazed round at a very peaceful sight. Mr Higgins sat in a rocking-chair outside the kitchen door, enjoying his pipe. The bears were lying on the river bank, quietly watching a little water vole. Muffin was with them and, as soon as she saw Ted, she ran barking to greet him.

The horses came out of the meadow to join the welcoming party and everyone said how pleased they were to see Emma looking so well.

'I feel wonderful,' she said, 'but it's good to be home.'

The first thing had to be a tour of the farm.

'But,' warned Mr Higgins, 'I must tell you that it isn't quite ALL good news, so I'll give you the bad news first,' and he told the farmer about the elm tree being struck by lightning.

To everyone's surprise Ted burst out laughing.

'That's not bad news,' he told them, 'it's GOOD news. That tree was nearly dead and it had to come down, because it wasn't safe. The storm has saved me the trouble and expense of getting it cut down *and* we've got a winter's supply of fire-wood.'

So, in a happy mood, they set off to show Ted and Emma that everything had been well-cared for. There was the spotless dairy and the contented cows that nuzzled Albert and rolled their brown eyes at him. The white chickens that ran to Digger when he called their names and the trays of eggs waiting to be collected. The tidy garden and the jars of honey. The boxes of fruit and the hay in the barn. Two sleek, well-groomed horses.

'And you've ploughed the field,' cried Ted, in delight.

'Not very well,' laughed Mr Higgins and told him about the Great Ploughing Match.

'It looks just fine,' Ted assured him.

'Shall we go and have supper now?' suggested Digger and led the way towards the house, but Albert hung back. 'Can you wait just a minute because I've got a bit of a surprise for you,' he said.

Every day, since the sheep market, Albert had been working at a secret something and now he was anxious to show them all what he had been doing.

He led the way across the bridge to where the pen stood on the far bank.

'Come here, Muffin,' he called. The little dog ran to him and sat down obediently at his feet. She did not bark and she did not jump up.

A hundred yards away, on the lower slopes of

the hill, about a dozen grazing sheep straggled about. Albert spoke to Muffin and she was off. But she did not run straight at the sheep, in her usual way; she went swiftly round them, crouching for a moment to watch and then backing off again, carefully circling the little flock, bringing them closer together. She made a sudden dash to collect a straggler and herded the sheep together again. Quickly the little dog brought the small flock down to the pen where Albert stood by the gate, ready to stop any sheep that tried to slip past.

Very cleverly Muffin brought the tight little group into the pen. Albert slammed the gate shut and looked round with a big grin on his face.

Muffin sat down quietly, looking just as pleased.

'Well!' gasped Ted. 'I never would have believed it. You really *are* a proper sheep dog! Here, Muffin.'

Muffin could not keep quiet any longer. She leapt and danced and licked the face of anyone she could reach.

Digger did not want to spoil Albert's fun but he had his own surprise to show off. 'NOW can we go in to supper?' he asked plaintively.

'Oh, yes, come on, Digger's got it all ready!' cried Albert.

They went into the kitchen and Emma was told to sit down and do nothing.

In the centre of the table stood a beautiful ham, a welcome-home gift from the pig-farmer. Next to it stood a bowl of salad. On a little blue plate was a pat of Albert's best butter, wearing a slightly crooked crown, to go with the potatoes simmering on the stove. Waiting on the dresser was a jug of thick cream and a dish of new plums, halved, stoned and cooked with honey.

Digger dished up the potatoes, Mr Higgins carved the ham and Albert poured glasses of cider.

Henry put his head in the door, cast his eye over

the feast and commented, 'I can see it's true what they say about farming and growing your own food.'

'What's that?' asked Albert.

'It is,' said Henry, 'the Good Life!'